The Passion Chronicles

The Last Week of Jesus' Life

By
Jonathan Srock

Jonathan Srock
87 Safe Harbor Lane
Smithmill, PA 16680
srockenator@gmail.com

www.Jonathansrock.com
www.solidrock831.com

If you enjoy this book, please visit my website and subscribing to do my email newsletter.

Signing up gives you the free gift of my short story collection.

Every month you'll be updated on my blog and everything that's happening.

Thank you for your support!

Visit www.Jonathansrock.com and subscribe

Table of Contents

Introduction

In the year of our Lord 33, a lowly carpenter turned rabbi enraged the ruler class of Israel. He paid for his insolence with his life. What follows are the Chronicles for each scandalous day of his last week, of the many lessons you can learn from his life and teaching,

The Passion Chronicles reveal what happens when the spiritual war between God and the devil breaks out into the natural world. Many people have said many things about this man. But the best decisions about people are made after hearing their story. Travel with me to a city called Jerusalem as the radical rebel introduces himself to the city for the last time.

In Like a Lion

Day One
Palm Sunday

"Hey, you there! What do you think you're doing?" The owner rushed over to the stables from the town square, "That's my property! Thieves!" The two men with sheepish faces like children with their hands caught in the cookie jar were standing aloof holding the reins of the newborn donkey, looking guilty as sin.

By the time the owner arrived to rescue his donkey from the vagabonds they were trying to explain themselves so they didn't end shackled in prison. The taller brute of a man trying to sound innocent and pass the buck to someone else, backing away from the donkey replied, "Please, sir, we mean no harm. We'll bring it right back. We just need to borrow it for the day."

The incredulous owner was about ready to blow a gasket, "You can't just borrow a donkey without even asking me! Get lost, you freeloaders!" He was motioning to some of the other men in the town square for assistance in getting rid of these unwanted criminals.

The smaller one chimed in, "But you don't understand! The Master said he has need of it and we assure you, we aren't thieves. We are only trying to do what our Rabbi told us to. He said you would understand." The two men looked like people who were tricked into a scheme unknowingly. It was as if they were realizing the ramifications of their actions for the first time. It finally dawned on them that other people would not understand what their Master had committed them to do.

Suddenly, the owner's entire countenance changed, "Oh, the Master? If you are referring to the man I think you are, then by all means take the animal." Without another word he turned around and walked back to the square.

The two men were so shocked that those simple words, those magical key phrases, were like backstage passes to a concert. All of a sudden it was okay to take the colt. No prison time. No public ridicule. They should try this kind of stunt more often. But the taller disciple could not resist and chased after the owner with curiosity, "Excuse me, sir! Do you know the Master?"

The owner stopped in his tracks, turned to the disciple and responded, "Yes! I was in the crowd when he fed more than I could count with a small amount of bread and fish! It is all the proof I need to trust his word that the donkey will be returned. If he needs anything more for his ministry, please let me know." And with that the owner continued toward his friends in the town square.

The tall disciple shrugged his shoulders and walked back to his friend. They proceeded on their mission to take the colt back to Jesus. It was the day after the Sabbath and the Feast of Unleavened Bread was upon them. It was going to be a typical Passover week and they were looking forward to the feast coming up. But it started out in the most peculiar way.

You see, they were just minding their own business earlier today when Jesus told them to do this task. They were hanging out with him on the Mount of Olives, headed to Jerusalem for Passover. Every good Jew celebrates Passover in Jerusalem if at all costs he can make it. This would be their third Passover since beginning to follow Rabbi Jesus years ago.

It was exciting to be part of something like his ministry, for there was none other like it. They would've never been chosen to continue studying the Scriptures with a Rabbi. Their memories were not good enough, so the other Rabbi's said to them. No one would choose them, but Jesus saw something in them they didn't even see in themselves.

Like any other time they were asked by Jesus to do something strange, they had learned by now that he knew what he was doing. They had resigned themselves to following his will no matter what it was. Besides, they wouldn't nearly have seen what they had in their lifetimes if they didn't obey the Master. This time was no different.

As they sauntered down the road, the colt trailing behind them, they mused over the past few years. It had been a wild ride! This Jesus was like no one else they had ever known. He did miracles, signs and wonders like no one else. And he taught with such authority! All the other rabbis would point to this ancient Rabbi or that, comparing each Rabbi to another while Jesus declared his teaching on his own authority rather than the authority of long gone rabbis from the past.

When they arrived at the Mount of Olives they were greeted by their friends and Jesus. The disciples piled on a few of their own coats to the back of the colt. He had never been ridden before. Without a word Jesus mounted the animal and they began the roughly 5 mile trek into Jerusalem. The disciples were not prepared for what was about to happen.

As they approached the city gate, there was quite a ruckus. A large group of Jesus' followers was lining the streets with giant palm branches. As the people cheered, they laid down coats and palm branches across the walkways and roads. The closer they got the louder the chants became, "Hosanna! Hosanna in the highest! Here comes the son of David, the Son of Man!" Of course, Jesus' followers were not the only ones to show up that day. Scowling on the fringes of the crowd were lawyers and religious leaders.

The disciples could tell this week was about to be different than every other week they had followed Jesus. The two disciples who had chased down the colt on their errand for Jesus exchanged glances of trepidation. It felt like they were walking into the biggest trap they had ever faced. They were glad they were with Jesus. It seemed no matter what these religious leaders had in store for him he was two steps ahead of them.

Jesus was almost stoic as he approached the city gate on the colt. He looked kingly, regal, as though he belonged in that spot. If Herod could see him now, he would be screaming at the soldiers to yank him off of that animal. It was bad enough the religious leaders exchanged glances that could kill. They could tell they hadn't seen the last of these scribes and Pharisees.

Jesus made his grand entrance, earning the name "The Lion of Judah." They would later look back and realize as he taught them that he was fulfilling a prophecy from Zechariah which said, "Say to the daughter of Zion, 'Behold, your king is coming to you, humble, and mounted on a donkey, on a colt, the foal of a beast of burden.' "

The crowds continued to cheer Jesus on to his destination but quieted down as he went toward the temple. Even the disciples didn't realize what Jesus was doing. But that was the last straw for the scribes and Pharisees. They were standing in the middle of the road blocking passage to the Temple.

"Halt! You cannot take that filthy beast anywhere near the Temple!" They were destined to clash with the Messiah because they could not see him for who he was. To them, he was a menace out of that podunk town of Nazareth. Everyone knew that nothing good comes from Nazareth! Who did he think he was coming to in such a fashion? They refused to let him pass.

This gave them time to hurl their accusations. The Pharisee in the middle of the group began his high and mighty speech, "Do you hear what they're saying about you? Do you intend to commit blasphemy right in front of us?"

Jesus smiled at them, "Out of the mouths of babes," he mused. "If they don't cry out, the rocks would."

"Who do you think you are?" The incredulous chief priests reveled their spot in the limelight. If only they could land a punch on this upstart Rabbi and send him back home away from their precious holy city it would've been a great day.

"Some say I'm a great prophet. Others say I am like John the Baptist. Everyone seems to have an opinion of me." Jesus got off of the donkey and walked up to them. Oddly enough, they did not stop him. As he approached them, they parted like the Red Sea back in Moses' time. He walked through them as if they were not even there.

Walking up some of the steps of the Temple, he turned around and began his discourse. With tears in his eyes he proclaimed, "Would that you, even you, had known on this day the things that make for peace! But now they are hidden from your eyes."

"For the days will come upon you, when your enemies will set up a barricade around you and surround you and hem you in on every side and tear you down to the ground, you and your children within you. And they will not leave one stone upon another in you, because you did not know the time of your visitation."

The disciples would later realize that Jesus was prophetically telling Jerusalem that it would not last much longer before the Romans would attack the city in battle and sack it.

The scribes, chief priests and Pharisees sneered at him and paid no mind to his warning. They decided the best course of action would be to wait and deal with him tomorrow. Besides, it seemed the whole world was going after him and they were truly outnumbered. They did their best work in secret anyway. This was not over and they were not even close to giving in and conceding their fight. They brooded as they pushed through Jesus' supporters. What was that he once said? Tomorrow brings enough trouble for itself? How true his words would become.

Cursing, Cleansing and Conspiring

Day Two
Monday

Warm breezes brushed against his face and beard and tasseled his hair as he walked dusty roads with his disciples. The sun rose from the ground highlighting the pinkish orange hues in the otherwise blue clear sky. Headed from Bethany to Jerusalem on a beautiful Monday morning, Jesus enjoyed the sunrise his Father had crafted just for him.

Despite three years of teaching about God and demonstrating the goodness of the Father, it seemed like he was not making too much headway. Sure, there were many, usually those who were healed or saw the miracles, who knew he was special. But the vast majority of his message was misunderstood.

He could understand what Isaiah felt like when his Father told the prophet that he would toil in obscurity. No matter how many times he demonstrated God's love for his people, they seemed not to see who he was or connect with his message of God's hope. Worse than that, Israel had been a big letdown. God chose this nation to show everyone else what he was like, but this never developed throughout history.

But Jesus was ever the optimist that his mission would be complete on this earth. And he knew the time was coming very soon. The kingdom of God was about to be inaugurated through him. He had explained it so many times with so many parables and now it was only days away. Jesus continued to enjoy the warm sun on his face and the Light breezes, not to mention the beautiful scenery. They had made this world so beautiful.

It was early in the morning and Jesus was becoming very hungry on the way. In the distance, he spotted some fig trees that were in leaf. Sure, it was early in the season and there probably weren't any figs yet, but he went to check anyway. He approached one of the trees still close to Bethany and combed the leaves with his hands. No matter how many leaves there were on the tree there was no fruit.

Disgusted with the results, Jesus cursed the fig tree, "May no fruit ever come from you again!" They continued on their journey and he listened to the background of the disciples discussing what had just happened.

Of course, Simon Peter was the first to pipe up, "It's not time for figs to be harvested yet. I wonder why he cursed the tree." Nathaniel mentioned that Bethany fig trees were notorious for coming in early and maybe he was expecting this one to be available since it already had leaves. They all continued to discuss it in hushed tones, afraid to simply ask Jesus why he cursed the tree.

They finally arrived in Jerusalem and Jesus went directly to the Temple. He was interested in beginning to teach there as he did in Galilee and other places throughout Israel. From the time of his youth when he was twelve debating the law with the priests and scribes until now, he was aware that not everything in the Temple was the way his Father would want it.

But this was his chance to right a wrong as he had been doing throughout his ministry. There was one thing in particular that always irked him when he visited. Today it was extremely noticeable knowing that he was coming to the end of his ministry. It was almost like retirement. There was nothing to lose. He knew the Father would approve.

After climbing the grandiose steps into the outer courts, where even the Gentiles were allowed to enter and pray, Jesus surveyed what was now called Herod's Temple, The second Temple erected by Ezra after the exile to Babylon. King Herod had added more ground to the Temple Mount and expanded the Temple to make it look even bigger and grander than when it was first built. He did this in an attempt to win over popularity with the Jews but got mixed results.

The first thing most people would notice when entering the Temple was the smell of blood mixed with smoke from the ongoing daily sacrifices. He distinctly noticed the sign warning of impending death for anyone who wasn't Jewish at the edge of the outer courts on the wall that separated these courts from the court of Israel. Most noticeable was the Most Holy Place, the columns of which rose above everything else in the Temple. This was the place that God's presence inhabited and no one was allowed to enter except the high priest once a year.

More than the stench of blood mixed with smoke, Jesus noticed them right away. Boisterous moneychangers along with those profiting from selling acceptable sacrificial animals, bulls, goats, sheep, birds and the like bristled his ears not only because they were noisy but because of what they were saying.

"Get your sacrificial animals here! Doves, sheep, goats, cattle! You name it we've got it, and the purest in the land!" One of the sellers was yelling so loud there was no way any Gentile, or Jew for that matter, could pray in the outer court. He knew for a fact that God never intended for Israelites to benefit off of travelers and sojourners who did not have the proper sacrificial animals.

As he looked at the other side of the Temple court the moneychangers were helping people exchange whatever money they had for the proper Temple tax. This would've been better placed outside of the Temple, for business and worship should not mix. Even worse than that, these moneychangers were actually shortchanging anyone who exchanged with them. The Temple coin never had a one-on-one comparison with any other money and so the moneychangers would make sure they would give just a bit less than the value of the currency they exchanged.

Jesus could not handle it anymore. He fashioned a whip with cords and began yelling louder than the moneychangers and sellers of sacrificial animals. When he began to act like a madman the people became frightened and he chased them out of the Temple courts, overturning the tables of the moneychangers and frightening the animals. All the while he was yelling, "My Father's house must be a house of prayer, not a den of robbers!"

In the back of his mind, Jesus knew this would infuriate the priesthood and all of the religious leaders, but this wasn't about them. This was about what the Temple should be about. None of these things belonged, and all of them were distractions from true worship by genuine worshipers. This wasn't about him and whether or not he got along with the religious leaders. This was about what was right in the Temple. The Temple had to be cleansed of the filth that crept in over the years unchallenged.

Elimelek, one of the chief priests, burst into the room shouting along with the murmur of the other chief priests. Caiaphas, the high priest, sat on the center chair which looked more like a throne than anything of the Sanhedrin, the governing spiritual body of Israel. The chamber filled with the chief priests and Pharisees, all clamoring for Caiaphas' attention.

"That blasphemer is sitting in our places and teaching the people, Pharisees! We must do something about it! If we let this keep on going, the Romans will take our power away from us and lay waste to our great city. They have warned us before of these Messiah types that rise up. We've already learned our lesson more than once that there is no king but Caesar. What are we going to do?" Elimelek was beside himself with anguish and rage.

Caiaphas attempted to calm the mob down. He stood up from his seat and began, "Settle down! Settle down. Nothing is going to happen to our great nation. I have already made sure of Dragon is now working rightthat. Do you think I am high priest for no reason? I have already put a prophecy out that this Jesus would die for the nation. We don't have to worry about him."

This calmed the crowd down for a moment. Caiaphas was able to continue, "We must find a way to make the prophecy come true. There must be something he has said along the way that we could charge him with. The trick will be that we are not allowed to commit capital punishment anymore. The Romans have made clear that only they can kill someone in our nation. Blasphemy will not hold up in their judgment. We must find something more incriminating than this."

The Pharisees and chief priests began to brainstorm. The Pharisees called in their spies who reported some of the teachings and sayings that Jesus had given over the past three and a half years. While all of the things that were said were convincing to the Jewish leadership, none of them would get the Romans on board.

Elimelek finally spoke up, "It appears we must bide our time and wait for the right moment to go in for the kill. God has to make many things work out in our favor. For one, the people are for him. They clamor after him and hang on every word of his vitriolic teachings. We don't have popularity on our side yet. Aside from this, we must continue to try to trap him so that he will say something incriminating in the Romans will want him dead as much as we do. Then, we need a snitch, someone who can lead us to him so that he can be arrested and tried for these crimes."

The general consensus of the room began to swing Elimelek's way. There was not enough evidence to convict Jesus in a Roman court of law. The Romans did not care about religious matters as long as they did not bother the Empire. They decided they would send out their spies to try to trap Jesus while he was in Jerusalem celebrating the Passover. They may not have their pound of flesh yet but every dog has his day.

Setting the Trap

Day Three
Tuesday

The road to Jerusalem traveled along the same route from Bethany. The weather was about the same as yesterday but we were worried about what the Master would do today. Yesterday he had taken us totally by surprise when he went into the temple. Talk about a way to enter Jerusalem for the last two days.

He always had a flare doing his ministry of dealing with the religious leaders but it was at a whole new level today. We knew that the pressure would only increase the more we showed up in Jerusalem. That didn't seem to bother him.

Suddenly, one of us shouted out, "Lord, the fig tree you cursed is withered!" And I turned to see Simon Peter pointing toward the trees on the side of the road. We all began to huddle around the bush the Lord had spoken to the day before and sure enough there were no figs on it. The leaves had withered into a brownish color and it drooped more than yesterday.

Jesus looked at it without any surprise and taught us, "If you have faith, anything you ask of Me will be done. You can say to this mountain, 'Be moved!' And it will be moved." We pondered this saying the rest of the way to Jerusalem. When we arrived, we followed Jesus back into the temple where he began to teach as he did yesterday. I heard a few of the scribes and elders murmuring among themselves and complaining about his teaching, because it was so different from what they were used to hearing from rabbis.

One of them stood up right in the middle of his teaching, "Jesus of the lowly Nazareth, from which nothing good comes, tell us by whose authority you do all these things and teach."

The Master sat there for a moment while everyone stood around him, a wry smile creeping across his face, "Tell me first, was the baptism of John from heaven or from man?"

We could see the wheels turning in their heads and smoke coming out of their ears as they discussed among themselves, "If we say from heaven, he'ill ask us why we didn't believe him. But if we say from man, everyone will stone us because they favored John." After several minutes of debate and deliberation, they turned to Jesus and replied, "We do not know from where it came."

The Master quickly responded like a trap going off on a mouse, "Neither will I tell you by whose authority I am doing all of these things." Game, set, match! Jesus picked up with his teaching again, offering some parables for us to chew on. "A father had two sons. He asked each of them to go into the fields and work. The first son told him he would not go but later changed his mind and went into the fields. The second son seemed obedient, 'I go to them now, sir!' But he did not go into the fields. Which one of these do you think the father was pleased with?"

You could hear a pin drop in the place. Then the crowd responded almost as if on cue, "The first one!"

Jesus responded, "You got it. Tax collectors and prostitutes and sinners may be saying no to God now, but they are more open to hearing about him as time goes on. It's religious leaders, like the scribes and Pharisees, who give lip service to God by saying they will obey him but don't actually do it when the sandal meets the dust. God looks at the heart more than the lips."

Then he continued, "I have another one. A man owned a vineyard and he took great care to plant and water it, providing protection with a fence and even preparing a wine press for it. Then he leased it to some tenants and went away on a trip. When time came to harvest, he sent some of his servants to gather the harvest from the tenants who worked the garden. But each one that he sent was abused by the tenants and beaten.

"So the owner decided to send his own son because he thought they would listen to him. The problem is that he sent his son and they receive the son by saying, 'Here is the master's son, the heir. If we kill him, we will own the land after the master dies. Come, let us kill the son!' What do you think the owner will do with those tenants?"

One of the boys of the families in the crowd piped up, "He will kill them and replace them with better tenants!" Everyone in the crowd burst out laughing.

Jesus chuckled, looked the boy in the eyes, and said, "That's right, young man." Then he addressed the crowd again, "Do you remember when the prophet said, 'The stone the builders rejected has become the cornerstone?' God's Kingdom will be taken from those who have abused it and given to people who produce good fruit."

The scribes realized immediately that he was talking about them. They murmured amongst one another, "How did he know about our plans to kill him?" They cowered away into the crowd just looking for an exit. Everyone watched them slink away like a dog tucks its tail between its legs.

We could've sat there for hours listening to Jesus teach, and he used several other parables to talk about God's Kingdom. We took a break to find something to eat for lunch but then Jesus was right back at it, teaching the people. The scribes and Pharisees came back for round two, attempting to trap Jesus once again.

They snuck in throughout the crowd and were listening to his parables. This time the Pharisees and scribes also brought the Herodians, a group of Jews sympathizing and collaborating with the Romans. The moment he finished, one of the lawyers stood up and said, "Teacher, is it lawful to pay taxes to Caesar or not?"

A gasp rushed through the crowd like running water and then a hush fell over them. Every eye was trained on Jesus as he responded, "Why are you testing me? Bring me a coin." One of the Herodians confidently brought a coin and handed it to the Master. He turned it over in his hand and then flipped it in the air. It turned over and over, landing on the back of his hand. "Whose image is on the coin?"

The Herodian looked at his hand, "Caesar's."

Jesus waited for a moment, probably for dramatic effect, and then uttered words that shocked the crowd, "Then give Caesar what's his and God what's God's." I thought back to my studies in Torah, to the first scroll of the Scriptures. God placed his image on every human being.

If I understood the Master correctly, he was telling us that we could give money to Caesar but it was most important that we give ourselves, our talents and our resources to God for his use.

The most enjoyable part of watching Jesus teach was glancing back at the Pharisees and scribes and seeing them cringe as every attempt to trap him failed. He outsmarted them every time.

The Sadducees, a group that didn't get out much because they were so attached to the Temple were next. They didn't believe in the resurrection like Jesus did. "Teacher, surely you understand Levitical laws. Moses taught us that if a man dies without having an heir, his brother should marry his widow and produce an heir for him. Now there was a man who died without a son, so his brother married his widow. But this man also died without producing an heir for his brother. The next brother married her as well and so forth for seven men in total. Now, in the resurrection, which one will be the widow's husband?"

This Sadducee told the story so that we would all think resurrection was a foolish idea. It seemed that the whole crowd was silent once again, pondering the conundrum. Jesus waited for a few minutes for each of us to think on the issue at hand. And then he spoke, "First of all, the third or fourth brother should've realized it's a bad idea to marry this woman." The crowd burst out laughing.

Then Jesus continued, "Your silly little stories belittle God's principles. You don't understand! Marriage is for this life. But in heaven, people will be like the angels who don't marry."

He spoke with such authority that the Sadducees slunk back into the crowd stunned. Before he could continue his explanation, one of the scribes stood up and asked, "Teacher, what is the greatest commandment?"

The Master responded, "That's an easy one. I will quote it for you, 'Love the Lord your God with all your heart, soul, strength, and mind.' This is the greatest commandment, and a second is like it. 'Love your neighbor as yourself.' If you live by these you will fulfill the whole law."

Stunned silence filled the room until the lawyer spoke again, "Teacher, you are right in what you say." Everyone stared at him, especially the other Pharisees and scribes. If looks could kill, he would be locked in a tomb. They couldn't believe he not only conceded to the Master, but also paid him a compliment!

Jesus locked eyes with him, "You're not far from God's Kingdom." He paused again and the lawyer slinked away into the crowd. Jesus addressed the Sadducees about the resurrection again. "I know you Sadducees don't believe in resurrection. You think only the Torah is inspired and ignore the other parts."

"It's my turn. Far after Abraham died, God declared that he 'is' the God of Abraham, Isaac and Jacob." He carefully stressed "is." "Tell me, why did God say he 'is' Abraham's God instead of 'was' his God? Wouldn't this mean Abraham, Isaac, and Jacob are still alive?"

If it got any quieter, you'd think everyone in the room was dead. Now it was the Sadducees' turn to look bad in front of the crowd.

The Pharisees boasted that they believed all parts of Scripture. The Master decided to put them in their place. "And what about you Pharisees? Have you not read in the Psalms of David, 'The Lord said to my Lord, sit at my right hand until I make your enemies of footstool for your feet.' You say this is addressed to David's son, the Messiah. But how does David address his son as 'My Lord'?" The Pharisees were speechless.

Jesus amazed everyone with his teaching and authority that day. He trapped the trappers and put them in their place. Everyone pondered everything he said. But he looked so sad for the religious leaders and Israel. They went away and continued to devise a way to catch him in his teaching.

I spent the journey back to Bethany for the night, all through dinner, and most of the night pondering everything he taught us. I knew I couldn't understand most of it on my own. But I also figured that the religious leaders and scribes probably knew what he was saying but refused to listen. How could such smart people not have a clue?

The Last Things

Day Four
Wednesday

A madman stormed into our Temple, drove out those trying to help with the sacrificial system and converting for the Temple tax, honorable establishments. He made us the bad guys in front of all of the people that usually come to us for teaching. This upstart from Nazareth thinks he's all that. He thinks it's funny what he makes us look trivial in front of the people.

We had been sick of him for years, but it got worse when he engineered his "triumphal entry" into Jerusalem with a handful of supporters. He made us the butt of every parable. But today was the worst. He fashioned himself as a prophet like the ancients. He acted like he knew how the world would end. We had it up to here!

Once again we found him teaching in the Temple courts. He was laying out his doomsday scenarios like an amateur. Why do the people clamor after him and go to him for advice? We're the ones who are trained in the law and prophets. Something must be done about him. We can't have him disrupting our way of life, not in our great city of Jerusalem. It curdles my blood just thinking about him sitting in our sacred Temple usurping our place of teaching.

As if he had not disgraced our Temple enough, this Jesus began telling us that the Temple would be destroyed! His disciples were better Jews than him, showing honor to our Temple by talking about how beautiful it is. But he couldn't stand it. He walked up to one of the giant foundation stones and put his hand on it. My ears hurt just listening to his blasphemy, "See this stone? Not one stone will be left on another. They will be torn down."

All I could think of was our ancestors' hard work in building the temple. He is so infuriating! At least he didn't stay in our precious Temple when he went out to the Mount of Olives to continue weaving his web of doom, gloom and despair. There he sat on a stone talking about the end of time. If only he knew his own end was near!

No matter how private he thought his conversation with his disciples was, I was eavesdropping on every word. His disciples treat him like some kind of Messiah but we've seen his kind before. They may think they are messiahs but they're just insane. And it's these dangerous madmen that put us in hot water with the Romans!

I can barely stomach making my report to this honored Sanhedrin and you, our high priest, Caiaphas. But I must go on with these disgusting details. This blasphemer continued to brainwash his delusional disciples who were asking him, "What will be the sign of your coming and the end of the age?"

The Nazarene responded, "You must first watch that you are not led astray by people claiming to be the Christ. They'll claim to come in my name but will be false Christ's." Ironic how this false Messiah was claiming others were false. They always do that. I guess when you think you're all that, you don't realize you're really nothing. Here today, gone tomorrow. Will take care of him!

He continued with grandiose predictions, "You'll hear of wars all the time, for the world will be in grave trauma until I return. But that's not the end even if it looks bleak." Can you believe he thinks something that happens every day shows its the end? At least he knows he's going way! But I digress.

But he wasn't done, "Nation will bicker with nation, and famines and earthquakes will be common. But these are just birth pangs. It's as if creation will be crying out for me to return." I almost fell off my stone. Calling him insane is too mild for him.

He just couldn't stop himself, "False prophets will be everywhere. They'll be working with the devil to do false signs and wonders to impress people. They are all part of Satan's move to get people's attention. Now you know what to expect." There are no words for this man. Unfortunately, my report is not finished, Great Caiaphas.

"You'll endure persecution, tribulation, and death. Everyone will hate you. Even amongst yourselves will be schisms and differences of opinion. The love of men who used to follow me will grow cold because it's easier to join the world than stay with me. Despite these setbacks, anyone who endures with me to the end will be saved, and the gospel will travel throughout the whole world! The Father can't wait until the harvest is ready so that I can return."

The delusions rolled off his lips like oil from a jar, "Beware! People will drive you off to court. But when you stand before them, my Holy Spirit will give you the words to speak. Families will be split over me. Everyone will hate you because of me. But remember, anyone who endures with me until the end will be saved!"

I assure you no matter how crazy this sounds, this report is accurate. I wanted to run from this madman but I want it to be complete for your sake. I wish that was the end but he was not finished, "When you see the abomination of desolation standing in the holy place of the temple, as Daniel the prophet warned, run for the hills! Don't waste time taking anything with you. I hope for your sake it's not during winter or on the Sabbath. Those days will be so treacherous that it's good God will cut them short."

As if disgracing our temple isn't enough, he thinks he knows what Daniel was talking about. I wish it stopped there, but he kept going, "Immediately after these tribulations will be signs in the heavens. The sun and moon will go dark and the stars disappear. Everyone will see the Son of Man in the clouds. Daniel prophesied this. I will gather everyone who trusted in me. Be alert! You know when it's harvest time and when the weather is changing. No one knows when I can come back except my Father. Watch for the changing of each season so you'll be ready."

He couldn't resist giving more parables. He talked about the times of Noah when people didn't listen to him about the flood. Then there is the wise servant who prepared for his master's return. But the wicked servant squandered the time. Jesus strangely moved from Noah to servants to ten virgins. There was something about having to wait for the bridegroom and having enough oil for their lamps. I may have drifted off a few times through this part.

He's preparing these followers for some catastrophic event that probably won't happen. But this man loves parables! He talked about being faithful as a servant. These three servants were given various amounts of money. The first two were careful to make more money for their master. But the third buried his money in the ground. The master was angry because he didn't even collect interest. The master must be this madman Messiah.

I am most elated to tell you he was finally getting tired of himself. The last thing they spoke of was the Son of Man returning and judging everyone. Of course he thinks he's the judge. He separated people into two groups, the sheep and the goats. This great judgment is supposed to happen while he sits on some throne. Now this guy fancies himself as a king! It all sounds fishy to me. We know that you, Caiaphas, are God's chosen judge.

You know my opinion of the man. He is a delusional maniac. He's talking about coming back, but it's very difficult to come back from death. Hopefully he runs away like the cowards of history, the messiahs that have come and gone. But we know that once a person is gone, they're not coming back.

In my opinion, dear Caiaphas and fellow esteemed colleagues of the Sanhedrin, we must deal with this threat now. The more he talks, the more full of himself he gets. Our nation is in grave danger! I hope something in my report will give you the information you need to put him away for good. I humbly submit my report to you for your review and action.

Final Preparations

Day Five
Holy Thursday

We stayed in Bethany on Thursday until lunch, getting invited to Simon the Leper's house. We shared a name in common, and I was honored when Jesus added "Peter" to mine. Everything was going well until a woman interrupted the party.

But Jesus was no respecter of persons. He treated everyone with common decency and cared about the heart more than the outside. She entered with an expensive alabaster jar. Jesus taught us not to judge, but she probably gained the expensive perfume through prostitution.

She darted toward Jesus, stood behind him, and unloaded the entire jar over his head and body. He wasn't fazed, as if he knew before she did it. The ointment almost drowned him as he reclined at the table. The woman pushed the jar aside and wiped his feet with her hair and tears.

Everyone around us was murmuring. Judas, our treasurer, was beside himself, "She wasted that whole jar! It's worth at least a year's pay and we could've given it to the poor." We learned later that Judas kept back money for himself from the coffers.

Jesus looked deeply into our eyes as if he could see our bare souls. Shaking his head in disappointment, he responded, "This woman has done a beautiful thing for me. You won't always have me with you. She's preparing me for burial."

Not a sound filled the room, but my mind was screaming, "Your burial? But I remembered Jesus predicting his death more than once. His teaching threatened the religious leaders. It wasn't far-fetched for them to kill him.

After lunch, we prepared for the Feast of Unleavened Bread. Every year we got the Passover meal ready. I asked Judas Iscariot on the way to come with me. "No, Simon. I have errands to run. I'll be there tonight." Without another word, he headed to the temple.

I thought nothing of it. We were too busy setting up the Passover meal. It reminds us of God's salvation from slavery in Egypt. Included in the meal is a roasted lamb, unleavened bread, four cups of wine, and bitter herbs. They represent parts of the story. Needless to say, it is a day of preparation.

We asked the Teacher where to celebrate this year. He sent us to a certain man in the city about a certain upper room. He would join us in the evening. I went to the marketplace, making sure to find the best ingredients. Other disciples searched the house for leavened bread, part of Passover tradition. Our ancestors left Egypt so fast they left the bread dough to rise.

When evening finally arrived I was still on my way. I was the last one to reach the upper room. It was my job to wash everyone's feet. I was so hungry I forgot about it. I approached the U-shaped table and reclined for dinner. Besides, I wouldn't be able to stomach any food if I got a whiff of Thomas's feet.

Before I could change my mind, Jesus walked over to the door, picked up the basin, removed his outer garment like a servant, and washed my feet. That was my job! I failed my Rabbi. I reclined in shame wishing he'd stop. My conscience couldn't take it anymore. "Lord, don't wash my feet. I should be washing yours!"

Jesus' eyes pierced my soul, "You don't understand what I'm doing for you now."

I retorted, sounding angrier than I was, "You will never wash my feet!" The guilt inside bubbled to the surface.

But Jesus didn't look angry, "If I don't wash your feet, you have no share with me."

I wanted him to know my heart because my mouth gets me into trouble. I cried out, "Lord, not only my feet, but my whole body!"

He explained further, "The one who baths is clean. Only feet get dusty on the journey. You are clean, although not everyone." I didn't understand he was talking about Judas. I was barely able to pay attention because my emotions were still volatile.

"I'm teaching you to be a servant because in my kingdom, servants are the greatest. The Romans lord their power over each other." He returned to the table.

Earlier during the dinner everyone was chatting, and it was hard to hear Jesus speaking. Being at the end of the table, furthest from him, I couldn't hear anything he was saying. I heard the other disciples say, "Is it I, Lord?" I asked the others to find out someone would betray him!

After the way I acted, I couldn't let this go. I jumped to my feet, "I'll never betray you, Lord! I'd be willing to die with you."

Jesus looked at me softly, "Simon Peter, before tomorrow begins, you will deny me three times before the rooster crows." I humbly sat down and continued eating. I didn't even see Judas leave during the meal. Jesus had told us that the person who shared his bread would betray him. It dawned on me later that Judas sat in the guest of honor seat beside Jesus.

It was time to drink the third cup of wine, the Cup of Salvation. Jesus took unleavened bread, "This is my body, broken for you in remembrance of me." He tore off a piece and passed it around to each of us. We ate the bread together.

Then he took the cup, "This is my blood poured out for you. Drink it, each of you, and remember me." We passed the cup and each drank. We sang the Passover song. I picked up the fourth wine glass, the Cup of Victory, but everyone stood and followed Jesus out of the upper room.

As he passed by, he said, "I won't drink of the fruit of the vine until I'm with you again in my Father's house." Jesus was leaving us. He celebrated the cup of salvation with us, and would provide salvation the next day. But victory will be celebrated in heaven at the Marriage Supper of the Lamb.

We headed to the Garden of Gethsemane where we often went when we visited Jerusalem. He taught us as we walked. Even though he talked about serving as greatness, some disciples argued about greatness anyway. But we didn't understand most of his teaching until later. He graciously reminded us of his earlier teaching.

He spoke to us as a friend instead of a disciple. He talked about loving one another and reminded us that those who sacrifice have the greatest love. He even talked about carrying a sword, and I was glad that I had mine on me.

He also talked about the Holy Spirit, our Helper. We passed a grapevine, and he compared himself to the vine, and we, his disciples, bear fruit. "Remain in me, because without me you can do nothing." He continued to teach until we arrived.

We entered the Garden and I will never forget his prayer, "I pray for them, for they are yours. I am no longer in the world, but they are. Father, keep them in your name. Sanctify them in your truth, your Word."

Three of us moved deeper into the garden with him. He looked different, seemed lonely and sorrowful. "My soul is heavy, even to death. Remain here, and watch with me." He moved to a solitary place as he often did.

I wish I could tell you what happened, but I fell asleep. It was a very long day. Later I found out he prayed with his face in the ground, "My Father, if it's possible, let this cup pass from me. Nevertheless, not my will, but yours be done."

A short time later, I felt the nudge of his hand and even in my groggy state I heard, "Can't you watch with me for even an hour? Watch and pray! It's easy to be tempted. The spirit is willing, but the flesh is weak." Then he returned to prayer.

All I remember after that is him waking us again. I felt terrible inside for not being there for him. He spoke again, "My hour is at hand. Let's meet my betrayer." I was still half asleep as we walked in the moonlit garden. I saw many torches, soldiers with gleaming helmets.

I recognized the man walking up to Jesus, Judas Iscariot! He whispered in Jesus ear, "Greetings, Rabbi," and kissed him on the cheek.

Jesus responded, "Friend, do what you came to do." Soldiers approached him, wrapping his wrists with ropes. My adrenaline shot up and I yanked my sword from its sheath. I aimed for the closest neck to me, whipping the sword around in the dark. I heard a scream as a man clutched his head where his ear had been. Blood streamed through his fingers as soldiers kept their distance from the the crazy man with a wild swing.

Jesus calmly approached the young man, bent down, picked up his ear, and placed it back where it belonged. The blood was gone! It was as if nothing happened. Jesus told me to put my sword away. They took him into custody and out of fear, all the disciples disappeared. I am ashamed to this day of abandoning him in his darkest hour.

I gained my wits just enough to follow them and know where they were taking him. Sure enough, it was the Sanhedrin. They wouldn't let him get away. It was time for their revenge.

I entered the court and warmed myself at the fire, trying to eavesdrop on the proceedings. False witness after false witness lied about him before the Council. Finally, two witnesses testified, "This man said he can destroy the temple and raise it in three days!"

Caiaphas stood up, overjoyed he found two witnesses to agree with each other. "Do you hear their accusations? Have you no answer?" Jesus was silent. In my mind, I pleaded for him to respond.

I couldn't hear much of the conversation because a servant girl recognized me and accused me of being one of Jesus' followers. I vehemently denied it, but others recognized me as well. Twice more I vowed I didn't know Jesus. The third time, I spoke harshest. And then I heard the crowing of a rooster in the distance. I ran out of the courtyard bawling.

I passed the temple in my defeat, but noticed Judas standing near some of the chief priests. I found a place to hide and listened to their conversation. Judas frantically pushed a money purse into their hands, "I thought you would arrest him! You're going to kill him. I didn't sign up for this!" For fear that they would see me, I snuck away.

When I was able to get myself under control, I returned to the courtyard only to discover Jesus received the death sentence. He refused to defend himself, and they took him to Pontius Pilate. The Romans didn't allow Israel's leaders to carry out the death penalty. They had to stick Jesus with a Roman death sentence.

I went to Pilate's castle to watch his trial. He was yelling in Jesus' face, "Are you the King of the Jews?"

Jesus responded, "You have said so." But he didn't defend himself despite the chief priests and the crowd. He wouldn't give in to Pilate at all. When the chief priests told him Jesus was a Galilean, he sent him to King Herod. The circus moved to King Herod's court since he was visiting Jerusalem for the Passover.

Herod couldn't wait to meet him, hoping he would perform a miracle for his enjoyment. But Jesus reacted the same way he did with Pilate. King Herod retaliated by letting his soldiers mock and beat Jesus. They put a robe on him and beat a crown of thorns on his brow. Since he wasn't much fun, King Herod sent him back to Pilate.

He took him into his private office to further question him. The last thing he wanted to do was make the Jews happy by crucifying this man. Besides that, he could tell Jesus was innocent. After many years in the Roman guard, he could spot a guilty man.

When he asked Jesus if he was a king again, he responded, "My kingdom is not of this world." Pilate was intrigued, but he couldn't show it to a prisoner. But as the interview wore on, he became more and more frustrated. He left the room in a fit of rage and decided he must appease the Jews to keep order.

There was a tradition to release one Jew before the Passover. He chose Barabbas, a hardened criminal and murderer, or Jesus. The crowd screamed Barabbas' name. To his dismay, Pilate let the murderer go. He allowed them to flog Jesus with the cat of nine tails, a leather whip with chunks of bone, rock, and metal in it.

With ultimate cruelty and joy in their work, the soldiers cracked the whip over his back ripping the skin off of his muscles. I couldn't stand to watch anymore. He was barely recognizable with the crown of thorns and the whipping done. His fate was sealed.

The Darkest Day

Day Six
Good Friday

The normally calm Via Dolorosa clamored with crowds yelling at the top of their lungs, "Crucify Him! Crucify Him!" The haggard shell of a man stumbled down the way, crimson streams of blood covering his body. His matted hair and patchy beard were barely recognizable as the Roman soldiers taunted the Jews in the crowd. He convulsed and then collapsed in the middle of the road, the crossbeam slamming into his back. The Romans plucked another man from the crowd and made him carry the cross.

On the hill called "The Skull" they slammed the man down on the beams and struck the nails through his hands into the wood. The man's bloodcurdling screaming could be heard above the crowds. As they pulled the cross into a standing position with ropes, it slid into the hole as the body bounced violently. There he hung for six hours from 9 AM to 3 PM. The innocent yet condemned Savior uttered seven sayings from that cross that reach through the corridors of time and speak even to us today.

Jesus hung there, his emaciated body the bridge between heaven and earth, God and humanity. When the sun set that night, the special Sabbath for Passover would begin. Hundreds of years ago, his people smeared a freshly sacrificed lamb's blood on their door posts to save them from the Death Angel. Now the hour of God's judgment for the world's sin had finally arrived. Here he was, the ultimate sacrificial lamb, his blood on the posts of the cross that would save the entire world.

Drifting in and out of consciousness, he thought back to those intimate moments with his disciples. He had come to show the world a true image of God. He demonstrated it through his teaching and action. The act he commits now is the deepest and most accurate image of God, how he loves and cares for humanity like a shepherd cares for his sheep.

He gazed down on the raging rioters shaking their fists, the high priest and his lackeys as they grinned like Cheshire cats at his demise. To his right and left, fellow prisoners, guilty while he was innocent, used their only breath to scream insults back at the crowds. Despite the pain it caused, he couldn't stay silent. He gathered his strength and took the deepest breath he could, "Father, forgive them for they know not what they do."

He closed his eyes and traveled to a different time. Earlier Jesus taught his disciples how to pray. Every eye was trained on him with curiosity as the words tumbled from his lips, "...And forgive us our debts as we also have forgiven our debtors." That prayer came with a warning that not forgiving others but forfeiting the Father's forgiveness.

Floating through memories, a slight smile crept across his face as his mind's eye focused on Simon Peter, "Lord, how often will my brother sin against me and I have to forgive him? Are seven times enough?" The look of dismay on his face was priceless when he replied, "Not seven times, but seventy times seven." Most of all he was proud of the growth of his disciples over the years.

His last great lesson on forgiveness happens now, as he hangs here taking most of his strength to speak and forgive his enemies. Though they derided, their tongues wagging from their mouths with rage, he couldn't deny his nature. He opened his eyes again. How long would he be able to endure these excruciating pains and fight the desire to slip away?

He resisted the urge to respond to everyone yelling and cursing at him. It was almost impossible to tune out the jeers from the criminal on his left. The man was so close and loud, "Save us, O mighty Messiah!" This stranger sarcastically mocked him. It didn't take his divine perspective to smell the man's disbelief.

But to his right, the barely audible voice of a broken man caught his ear. He looked at the other criminal. The moment Jesus looked his way, he tried to hide his face with little success. Jesus listened to his heart, "... We are guilty and deserve death, but this man is innocent." Then he bowed his head and closed his eyes. "Jesus, remember me when you enter your kingdom."

Compassion welled up in the Savior, "Today, you'll be with me in paradise." Images of his Father walking with Adam in the cool of the day in the midst of Eden flooded his thoughts. Those were precious times before evil grasped the human heart in a naked attempt to rip God's heart from Him and steal away His creation, sinking its filthy claws into God's glorious masterpiece. The Father's plan to win creation back with his Son had arrived!

The man's eyes shot open with utter surprise. His face glowed as the calm of eternity seeped through his body. Peace rushed over him as he realized nothing could steal Jesus' gift. He resigned himself to physical death, the doorway to eternal life. Jesus could see his heart of gratitude by reading his lips.

More time passed, and Jesus opened his eyes toward the crowd below. His mother, Mary, surrounded by her friends, was so close she could touch the cross. As he glanced to his left, he saw his disciple John consoling Mary. John deeply loved him and his family. As her eldest son, Jesus was responsible for her care.

Overwhelmed with compassion temporarily numbing the sting of pain, Jesus knew what he would do. He did what any dying son would do. His mind wandered to a happier time when his mother and brothers were demanding the return home from teaching the crowds. He remembered looking into his disciples' eyes, "... And who are my mother and brothers? Those who do my Father's will."

He gathered strength again and spoke to his mother for the last time, "Behold your son; behold your mother." Both Mary and John quizzically looked up at him and then at each other. John embraced Mary who continued to weep over Jesus. He looked up at the cross, "Master, she is in the best of hands and in my heart."

At noon, the sun disappeared and the darkness expanded across the sky. Fulfilling Scripture, soldiers haggled over his clothing, gambling for the most prized possession, a seamless linen garment. Electricity shot through his veins from his nail pierced hands. Out of pure anguish, he cried out in Aramaic, "Eli, Eli, lama sabachthany," which means, "My God, My God! Why have you forsaken me?"

For the first time Jesus felt alone. The crowd speculated on his words. Some thought he called the prophet Elijah. But the people misinterpreted his allusion to the ancient twenty-second Psalm that prophetically spoke of his crucifixion. He felt so alone. No one understood him or his teaching. In his final hours, the futility of his preaching to a world that neither understood nor cared was most aggravating and caused him deep sadness.

Whether minutes or hours passed by he didn't know, but the finish line was in sight. There was still more to do, so he called out, "I thirst!" to fulfill prophecy. Earlier a Roman soldier offered him a spot full of painkilling vinegar and sour wine out of sheer pity.

The instant he tasted it, he realized it was a sedative! He must suffer the full brunt of pain and anguish. He must experience the depths of human suffering possible. Only through such suffering would he understand every cry in the darkness from his children. He pulled his face away from that sponge and spit out the poison, the easy way out.

But when he tasted the sour wine, it was not the same sedative. He drank so he could finish his mission. He was just a few words away from home. He mustered strength, filled his lungs and cried out with glee, "It has been finished!"

The mission was an unprecedented success! He left his throne and came to earth to offer God's salvation to every human being who would accept and follow him. Although Jesus' arms sagged, his heart soared. Despite the piercing pain Jesus was suffering the devil couldn't win now. With every wheezing breath of his weakening lungs, Jesus was restoring God's creation to him.

It was finally time to return to his Father. With satisfaction in his voice, he spoke his final words. "Father, into your hands I commit my spirit." He lay down his life to set into motion the proof of his victory. With his last breath, the Holy Spirit could be released into the hearts of humankind. Knowing he would be in his welcoming Father's arms, Jesus yielded his spirit.

No one could take his life from him because an innocent man is free from sin and it's death sentence. Jesus chose to give himself to death to reverse the curse on humanity. Because he loves every person, Jesus was willing to drink the dregs of suffering worth every agonizing moment.

The Shut-Ins

Day Seven
Saturday

Yesterday, our Master died, our hopes and dreams with him. Thursday night we abandoned him, running for our lives. We all felt guilty. But what could we do? Soldiers captured him. We only had two swords. And we didn't think they'd really try to kill him. But that's exactly what happened.

Oh the dread of Friday! If we came near the cross, they'd recognize us. There he was, high and lifted up. He must've felt abandoned as we watched from afar. Not only did we run away from him in his darkest hour but we didn't have the guts to come near him at death. Only John was at the foot of the cross. The rest of us were invisible.

We were more concerned with our own lives. Of all the disciples, I had the hardest time trusting Jesus. I could say I'm the skeptic, the one who doubted the longest before believing. I even saw his miracles and teaching with my own eyes and ears.

There we were the day after he died. As soon as his final cry, we fled to the safe haven of the Upper Room. Afraid the Roman soldiers would execute us the same way, we disappeared from public life. That thick door with its solid lock made us feel safe whether we were or not.

Before we ran we had to know where they buried his body. We trailed in the shadows as Joseph of Arimathea took the body to his own tomb. We would have to give him a proper burial. Everything was rushed because The Sabbath and Passover were starting.

They wrapped him in linens but didn't prepare his body with spices and ointments. After the Sabbath, the women will tend to him. We feel trapped like our ancestors were slaves in Egypt during the Passover that celebrates their salvation and freedom. And we have good reason to be afraid. Jesus clashed with the religious leaders every time he taught.

They posted Roman guards at the tomb, probably to keep us from trying something. If you learn anything from your youth, it's not to mess with Roman soldiers in an occupied province. They are ruthless! For the second time, we abandoned Jesus for the Upper Room. So we sit up here second-guessing ourselves and throwing a pity party. We let him down again.

We don't know what to do. Some are talking of returning to their former occupations, fishermen, tax collectors, and others. I'm thinking of moving, perhaps to a small island where no one knows me. We took a big risk following Jesus. We believed in him, but his death was so brutal and final. The revolution of God's kingdom is lost to us.

The despair we feel is unbearable. We still believe all of his teachings. Many of us are recounting his teachings and we realized he talked about being raised on the third day. Oh if only that was true! I will never forget him. He brought me out of my shell. I was always timid and skeptical but he made me believe in something, in him.

The last night of his life, he talked about peace and persecution. He was encouraging us, but he needed encouragement. But we abandoned him instead. It's our fault he was alone! We might as well have been Judas. We thought it was every man for himself, but Jesus is the one who suffered.

We left him in the garden to be arrested by the Temple guards to save our own skin. I guess I'm paranoid, thinking they knew who I was and where I am now. Simon Peter might be the only one feeling worse than me. He went to Jesus' trial and ended up denying him three times. I don't know if he'll ever bounce back.

Jesus entrusted John with his mother, Mary. We all agree he had a special relationship with the Master. Someone started calling him the disciple Jesus loved, and it stuck. Although Jesus loved all of us, he had his closest relationship with Peter, James, and John.

We are gathered around a table with food on it but no one can eat anything. The women disciples graciously prepare these meals and sneak them into the room. I can't even eat out of guilt. Everyone keeps talking about Jesus in the past tense. He was standing before us in the garden not a day and a half ago.

Andrew spoke up with the profound thought, "It's ironic we saw Jesus raise Lazarus and that beautiful little girl from the dead. But now he has passed." Everyone began recounting the miracles we witnessed. We kept coming back to his predictions of his resurrection.

The grandest of stories would be told if Jesus did rise from the dead tomorrow. We should expect it, but even believers have doubt from time to time. We cowered behind a locked door with a sliver of hope.

It's so strange to not be celebrating the Passover in public. I've never done this before! But these are special circumstances. Many of us half expected to hear Jesus knocking on the door.

How can we teach as his disciples? Anyone would say, "Your Rabbi died for these teachings. Why should I follow them?" To be hung on a cross is a disgrace. Everyone in Jerusalem knows what happened to Jesus. Going back to our old lives dishonors our Rabbi.

I don't know how long we'll stay in the self-imposed prison. We can't stay here forever. After the Passover celebrations are finished, we will have to find another hiding place. I hate to sound like I'm giving up, but what other options do I have?

I'm disillusioned. I was so sure Jesus was the Messiah. He taught with authority and did miracles. But he didn't rise up against Rome or bring an earthly kingdom. He must've felt alone yesterday, but we feel alone today. I long for his predictions of resurrection to happen!

Some of the women will go to the tomb tomorrow. They are less well known than us. They were in the background of Jesus' ministry. We are supposed to be men, but we are acting like children. We'll never live this down. What a nightmare! I haven't been able to sleep. The terrors we watched Jesus suffer make us feel trapped. Jesus' peace is the furthest thing from our souls.

I lost a friend, not just a Rabbi. I'm lost without him. The good news of his joyous kingdom is gone. We all need a dose of hope. Without him, we are nothing.

Oh Happy Day!

Day Eight
Resurrection Sunday

The sky had that eerie hue right before the dawn. It was Sunday morning. I ran ahead of the group of women to get the gardener to help with the stone. We had prepared spices and ointments after the Sabbath to properly bury Jesus.

I knew I couldn't roll a tombstone away myself. It usually took several men! We were bringing spices and ointments to properly bury the Savior we loved.

The rising sun colored the rocks and played with the shadows. I went to the place the disciples saw Joseph of Arimathea bury Jesus. I saw a hole in place of the stone. My heart beat faster and faster as I ran to the tomb. Did they move him? Did someone take him away?

I stood in front of the tomb and the other women caught up with me. We peered inside but the body was gone! We panicked. Where was our Lord? We frantically search for someone, anyone, to explain what happened. But no one was around.

Suddenly, two men appeared in dazzling white clothing. They startled us, and we were afraid and in shock. They asked, "Why are you looking for the living among the dead? Jesus isn't here. He has risen!" They told us Jesus would meet the disciples in Galilee, but we were too surprised to hear it.

It finally dawned on us that they were angels. I couldn't believe it. I thought I was having a dream. The other women, Mary, James' mother and Salomé started walking back to Jerusalem to tell the disciples. I lingered in a daze feeling more lost than ever.

Then I saw him, dressed in white and resembling the glowing angels. I thought I finally found the gardener. I ran to him, "Excuse me, sir. The body that was in that tomb over there, do you know where it is?

He turned toward me but didn't speak. I started repeating myself out of desperation. I don't remember if what I said made any sense. It might've sounded like, "Please, sir! They crucified my Lord just three days ago but because of the Sabbath my friends and I could not come. I must know where he is!"

He couldn't possibly understand how much I cherished our Lord. He changed my life and I've followed him ever since. I had the worst reputation before I met him. In my former life I was a, um, lady of the night. When I met Jesus, I was entertaining seven demons. I wasn't always myself. But everything changed when Jesus set me free!

They took Jesus away from us and killed him. We were lost without him. While I was trying to explain myself to this person, one word cut through the clutter. The "gardener" looked into my eyes and said, "Mary!" I stopped in my tracks. That voice! I know that voice! That's the voice of Rabboni, my Jesus!

The second I realized it was Jesus, I dropped to the ground and reached for his feet. He immediately cautioned me, "Please don't touch me yet! I haven't been to my Father." I didn't know what that meant, but I obeyed him. It was true! Jesus was raised to life again!

Beside myself with joy, I listened to every word. He told me he would meet the disciples in Galilee, as the angels had said. I turned to go to Jerusalem, then turned back to express my joy to him, but he had already disappeared. I ran to catch up with the other women.

Running as fast as I could, I finally met them. "Ladies! Ladies! I've seen Jesus!" They turned to see me barreling down the road right at them. As I passed them, everyone started to run. I kept telling them about what I saw, "He said the same thing the angels said. He will meet the disciples in Galilee."

We got to the Upper Room in record time. We knocked on the door, "It's us! Mary Magdalene, James' mother and Salomé! Let us in!" We finally heard the lock click and the door swung open. We burst through the doorway, "He's alive! Jesus is alive!" The disciples stared at us blankly. They probably thought we were crazy.

I recounted what happened at the tomb. Unfortunately, a woman's word doesn't even hold up in court. Finally Peter and John flew out of the room to check our story. The others continued politely listening, as if we were their mothers.

When Peter and John returned, John told us he beat Peter there. Peter was reluctant to admit it. He countered with, "But I was the first to walk in the tomb," a satisfied look on his face. When they looked in, the tomb was empty and his burial clothing was neatly folded. If people stole the body, they wouldn't have folded up his garments.

Finally they believe me. But I wasn't the only one. Two disciples going to Emmaus later told us they saw Jesus that day. They also didn't recognize him at first. They were discussing Jesus' crucifixion when he walked up to them. They didn't recognize him until they broke bread together, just like at the Lord's Supper Thursday night. Then he revealed the Scriptures about himself.

Later that night, he appeared suddenly in the Upper Room behind a locked door. He showed them his hands and side for proof. Thomas was absent but would later put his hands in Jesus' wounds. Even though he spent forty days with us before ascending to the Father, we celebrate this day that he rose from the dead.

When he died on the cross, he was the innocent sacrificial lamb in our place. His innocence won victory over sin. When he rose three days later from the dead, he won victory over death.

His victory guarantees eternal life for everyone who believes in him. Never forget to lavishly celebrate Resurrection Day! It completes our salvation and eternal destiny! To Jesus be the glory!

About the Author

Rev. Jonathan Srock is an ordained minister with the Assemblies of God for 10 years. He received two Bachelor's degrees in Biblical Languages and Pastoral Ministries, as well as a Masters of Divinity from Assemblies of God Theological Seminary. He was privileged to be the Lead Pastor of New Life Assembly in Shillington, PA for four years before suffering sudden paralysis. Jonathan has been a Christian for about 30 years.

His passion is to help imprint the character of Christ through teaching and preaching God's Word. Rev. Jonathan is part of the PennDel Ministry Network. He is a quadriplegic and lives in Central PA with his parents. He enjoys preaching in local churches, writing books, blogging, and answering questions about God and the Bible. He also enjoys reading, watching sports, and geeking out over computers in his "spare" time.

Made in the USA
Coppell, TX
20 February 2021